The Puppy Collection

Nutmeg All Alone

Susan Hughes

Illustrated by
Leanne Franson

Scholastic Canada Ltd.
Toronto New York London Auckland Sydney
Mexico City New Delhi Hong Kong Buenos Aires

Scholastic Canada Ltd.
604 King Street West, Toronto, Ontario M5V 1E1, Canada

Scholastic Inc.
557 Broadway, New York, NY 10012, USA

Scholastic Australia Pty Limited
PO Box 579, Gosford, NSW 2250, Australia

Scholastic New Zealand Limited
Private Bag 94407, Botany, Manukau 2163, New Zealand

Scholastic Children's Books
Euston House, 24 Eversholt Street, London NW1 1DB, UK

www.scholastic.ca

Library and Archives Canada Cataloguing in Publication
Hughes, Susan, 1960-, author
Nutmeg all alone / Susan Hughes ; illustrated by Leanne Franson.
(The puppy collection ; 8)
Issued in print and electronic formats.
ISBN 978-1-4431-4652-4 (paperback).--ISBN 978-1-4431-4805-4 (html).--
I. Franson, Leanne, illustrator II. Title.
III. Series: . Hughes, Susan, 1960- Puppy collection ; 8
PS8565.U42N88 2016   jC813'.54   C2015-907517-3
                                                       C2015-907518-1

Thank you to Dr. Stephanie Avery, DVM, for her puppy expertise.

Cover Credits:
Cover: Cover photo © PeeWee/Westend61/Corbis
Corners: © Freeroot/Shutterstock.com; Logo: © Mat Hayward/Shutterstock.com;
© Michael Pettigrew/Shutterstock.com;
© Picture-Pets/Shutterstock.com. Background: © Anne Precious/Shutterstock.com;
© dip/Shutterstock.com. Back cover: pendant © Little Wale/Shutterstock.com.

6 5 4 3 2 1   Printed in Canada   121   16 17 18 19 20

MIX
Paper from
responsible sources
FSC® C004071

To Elizabeth Savary-Gosnell, a kind and conscientious crossing guard and dog-walker extraordinaire

CHAPTER ONE

Kat was surrounded by puppies. There was a basset hound puppy right at her feet. She held a cute little poodle and an adorable bloodhound in her arms. And there were three puppies in her lap: a Samoyed, an Irish wolfhound and an Australian shepherd.

More puppies were playing close by.

The school bell had rung, but Kat hadn't moved. She was sitting in the schoolyard with

her back against a tree. She had her hood up and her mittens on. Her eyes were closed.

"Kat? Kat, are you all right?"

Kat's eyes remained closed. She smiled, still daydreaming about puppies.

"Kat? Are you okay?"

Okay? Of course, she was okay. In fact, she was more than okay! Her parents had finally given in. They were letting her get a puppy. Now the only problem was choosing what breed she wanted. How could she choose? They were all so sweet.

"Kat. Kat!"

Kat sighed. She didn't want to end the daydream. In real life, she wasn't allowed to get a dog. Her parents said they didn't have enough time to look after one, even though Kat promised she would do everything.

But when Kat opened her eyes, she blushed. Owen was standing there looking at her with a worried expression on his face.

Many of the other kids in Kat's grade four/five class were already lined up at the school doors. Kat's friend Grace was in line. But not Kat. She had gone home for lunch and had come back early. But instead of playing with her friends, she had ended up sitting under the tree and daydreaming for a few minutes.

Owen kept looking at Kat. Owen was in Kat's class and he was her friend. Some of the girls at school teased Kat about Owen. They said he liked her just because he got tongue-tied when Kat was around. He had been playing ball with his friend Matthew, but then he must have seen that Kat didn't get up when the bell rang. Or open her eyes.

"Hey, Owen!" yelled Matthew from across the yard. He threw a baseball up in the air and caught it. "You coming, O?"

"Are you . . . are you okay, Kat?" Owen asked.

"Of course." Kat said. "I was just resting."

She couldn't tell Owen about her puppy daydream. She couldn't tell him about the Puppy Collection either. That was the scrapbook that she made with her friends Maya and Grace. All three girls thought puppies were the best thing in the world, but none of them had one. For fun they collected photos of their favourite puppies or they made drawings of them. They wrote descriptions, too. They put it all in the scrapbook. It was like having their own collection of puppies, and it helped them remember real puppies that they had met.

Owen was her friend, but if she told him

about her daydreams or the Puppy Collection, he might tell the other kids. They might laugh at her, Maya and Grace.

Just then Kat saw Maya hurry into the schoolyard. The two friends weren't in the same class this year, but they usually ate lunch together. Today, however, Maya had had a dentist's appointment at noon. Her father had just dropped her off.

The school bell rang again.

"Last bell, O," yelled Matthew. "Come on! Don't let your girlfriend make you late."

Now Owen blushed.

"I'm fine, Owen. Go ahead. Really," said Kat, feeling awkward.

Owen stood for a minute without moving.

"See you in class," Kat said.

"Kat-kay," said Owen. "I mean, kay-Kat." He shook his head. "I mean, okay, Kat." Owen ran to catch up with Matthew.

Kat hurried over to Maya. Her friend had short black hair, which she clipped back. She was very dramatic and so much fun to be around. She made everything special.

"Chatting with the boy with the lovey-dovey eyes again, Kat-nip?" teased Maya. "I'm beginning to wonder if everyone's right, and you *do* like him!"

"Very funny," said Kat. The girls at school teased Kat about Owen to be mean. Maya only teased her in fun.

Maya pulled on Kat's jacket. "Let's go. *Pronto.* Or we'll be late." The girls began running toward the school. "Oh, and Dad says yes, I can come to Tails Up after school."

Now Kat smiled. Her Aunt Jenn owned a dog-grooming salon called Tails Up. She also boarded puppies there, usually one at a time. Aunt Jenn's receptionist, Tony, answered phone calls, made appointments and took care of payments. But Aunt Jenn often needed extra help with her puppy boarders. That's when she called on Kat and her two pals to lend a hand. The girls were always keen to come by after school or on weekends to play with the puppies or walk them.

Just that morning, Aunt Jenn had called Kat before school. Tails Up had a new puppy coming to stay. Aunt Jenn wondered if the girls could come by after school.

Kat asked Grace and Maya in the schoolyard that morning, and the girls promised to check with their parents at lunchtime.

"I'm glad you can come, Maya. That's great!" said Kat. "Let's hope Grace can, too!"

"*Ciao, bella*," Maya cried, as she headed off toward her class's line. Maya was always trying

out words and phrases in different languages, just for fun.

Then Maya stopped. "Hey, Kat!" she called. "Your joke of the day: What breed of dog will laugh at any joke? What's the answer?"

Kat grinned and waggled her finger at Maya. "You know I can't tell you before I tell Grace. You'll just have to wait until we're all together!"

"Tell me now!" Maya demanded, with her hands on her hips. She put on a big pout.

"Sorry," teased Kat. "Got to go!"

"The worst. You are the worst, ever!" complained Maya. But then she made her mouth go sideways and did funny googly-eyes at Kat before disappearing through the school doors.

Kat giggled and quickly ran to join her own line.

CHAPTER TWO

As soon as Kat got to class, Grace told her that she could go to Tails Up after school, too.

"Oh, good!" said Kat. "I'm excited to meet the new puppy, aren't you?"

"So excited!" said Grace. She sat at the desk next to Kat. Grace had soft brown eyes. Her red hair was in two long braids. They reminded Kat of Anne from *Anne of Green Gables*. "Did your aunt tell you what breed the puppy is?" she asked.

Kat shook her head. "Aunt Jenn just said that she was really sweet and we would love her." She grinned. "It doesn't seem possible that anyone could love puppies as much as you and I and Maya do . . ."

"But I think your aunt does," said Grace, finishing Kat's thought.

The afternoon flew by. When school was over for the day, Kat and Grace grabbed their backpacks and their jackets. They raced outside to meet Maya. She was waiting for them at the school entrance.

"The new little puppy awaits us," Maya said dramatically. "Let us depart henceforth to Tails Up!"

The girls chatted as they hurried down the street. After a few blocks, they cut through the park toward Grace's house. It was on the street that ran down the far side of the park. Grace and her family had moved to Orchard Valley just after school started. Before that, Grace had lived on a farm.

When they reached Grace's house, Grace ran in to drop off her backpack. In a few minutes she was back, and the three girls continued on their way.

Maya suddenly frowned. "You. Joke girl." She pointed at Kat.

Grace couldn't help grinning. She knew what was coming.

"We need the answer. And we need it now," Maya demanded.

"What breed of dog will laugh at any joke?" Grace chimed in, reminding Kat. "You never told us the answer!"

"And it better be hilarious," warned Maya. "It is just not fair to torture us by asking the joke in the morning and then making us wait all day for an answer that is . . ." She looked at Grace. "Tell her, Grace," she said.

"Horrible," said Grace.

"Terrible," added Maya.

"Unbelievably bad," said Grace.

"So," continued Maya, as they turned the corner. "Spill. What breed of dog will laugh at any joke?"

Kat looked at Grace and then at Maya. "You can't guess?"

The two girls rolled their eyes at Kat.

"I think it's pretty obvious," said Kat, trying not to laugh. "The breed of dog that will laugh at any joke is a . . . chi-ha-ha."

"So bad!" Grace cried.

"All-time worst!" Maya gasped.

Kat's two friends began to chase her while they giggled. She ran ahead of them, grinning.

After a while, the girls reached the main street. They sprinted past a restaurant, the barber shop, the bank and several stores. When they reached Tails Up! Grooming and Boarding they stopped and caught their breath. The bell on the front door jingled as they went inside. Tony, the receptionist, waved to them from behind the front desk. He was speaking to a client who held a newly groomed black-and-white teacup poodle in her hands.

Kat waved back. Then she glanced around the waiting room. Two clients were waiting for Aunt Jenn. A young man sat with a black standard schnauzer at his feet. A woman in a woolly white jacket and hat sat with a fluffy black-and-white Lhasa Apso on her knee.

Kat nudged Maya when she saw the woman. Some people made Kat and Maya think of certain dog breeds. Sometimes dog owners and their dogs looked like one another.

Maya giggled. "Twins," she said to Kat.

Grace was also giggling, but for a different reason. The client at the front desk was holding her tiny teacup poodle so that she was eye level

with Tony's cat, Marmalade, who sat on the counter. Tony's fifteen-year-old tabby cat went everywhere with him. She came in to work with him each day and sat on the counter glaring down at the dogs. Now Marmalade rose to her feet. With her back arched, she stalked down the counter. She curled up in a disgruntled ball with her back to the friendly teacup poodle.

"Poor Marmalade," Grace joked. "She has to put up with so much!"

Kat and Maya grinned. They all knew that Marmalade was snobby on the outside, but she was a marshmallow on the inside.

"Girls," called Tony. "Jenn just finished grooming Ms. Tinkerbell and she has slipped into the doggy-daycare room to check on the new boarder. Do you want to join her there?"

"You bet," said Kat. "Thanks, Tony!"

The three girls hurried down the hallway and into the doggy-daycare room. It had a large fenced-in area where dogs could play. A staircase led to Aunt Jenn's apartment and a big room for puppy training. There was a door that led outside to a fenced-in yard. There were four large dog kennels along one wall.

"We're here, Aunt Jenn!" cried Kat, as they entered the room.

"Oh, this is such good timing!" Aunt Jenn wore her pink grooming coat. As usual her brown hair was pulled back into a ponytail. In her arms, she cuddled a little white-and-chestnut puppy. "I am just checking on our newest little guest. Girls, let me introduce you to Nutmeg."

16

The girls hurried over.

"Oh, what a pretty face!" cooed Grace.

The puppy had chestnut ears and chestnut markings around her eyes. She had a wide white blaze that ran down the centre of her face. Her tail was long and had a white tip.

Kat gently stroked Nutmeg. Her fur was smooth as silk. Her ears felt like velvet.

"Nutmeg is ten weeks old," said Aunt Jenn. "She is a Cavalier King Charles spaniel."

"A Cavalier King Charles spaniel," Maya repeated slowly. "What a name!"

"It is certainly a mouthful." Aunt Jenn smiled.

"What does *Cavalier* mean?" asked Grace.

"A Cavalier was a knight who supported King Charles the First," said Kat. "He was the king of England, back in the 1600s. The next king, King Charles the Second, really liked this breed of spaniel. He always had two or three with him."

"So the breed was named after King Charles
the Second?" said Grace.

Kat nodded. "Yup."

Maya and Grace grinned at each other. Kat
knew so much about dogs that Maya called
her Einstein. Kat read lots about dogs on the
Internet and in her favourite book, *Dog Breeds of
the World*. Kat hoped one day she would know
as much about dogs as her aunt did.

"Would one of you like to hold little Nutmeg?"

Aunt Jenn asked. "How about you, Kitty-Kat?" That was her special nickname for Kat.

Kat's heart fluttered. *Of course* she wanted to hold the adorable puppy, but she knew her friends did, too.

"Let Maya go first," said Kat.

Maya smiled gratefully at Kat and held her arms out for Nutmeg.

"Oh, look at you," Maya murmured, as she cuddled the puppy. But the puppy didn't even look up. She just stared ahead of her with sad brown eyes.

"So, here's the scoop." Aunt Jenn popped her bubble gum. "Nutmeg's owner, Tracy Gulian, had to leave this morning to visit her sick mother. She arranged for her neighbour to go over and feed her two cats, Oliver and Buddy. But she couldn't find anyone to look after her new puppy. So Nutmeg is staying here for four nights, until Sunday."

Aunt Jenn smiled. "Girls, would you be able to come by and play with Nutmeg after school for the next two days and on Saturday? It would be wonderful if you could."

"I can," said Kat.

Maya and Grace said they would check.

"Righty-roo," said Aunt Jenn. "Thank you so much, girls."

Then Aunt Jenn showed the girls which kennel Nutmeg was using. She pointed out Nutmeg's leash, and she explained what treats the puppy could have.

Kat listened to her aunt, but she also watched Nutmeg. The puppy didn't wiggle with excitement. Her eyes didn't sparkle. She didn't struggle to be set down so she could run around. She didn't act like any of the other puppies Kat had helped look after at Tails Up.

"Aunt Jenn, is Nutmeg all right?" Kat said. "She seems so quiet."

"Many puppies take time to settle when they are away from home," said Aunt Jenn. "Nutmeg hasn't been here very long. I'm certain she'll cheer up after you three spend some time with her."

Aunt Jenn gave a gentle tug on Nutmeg's ears and then hurried back to the grooming studio.

"I hope you're okay, puppy," said Maya.

CHAPTER THREE

Maya carefully handed the puppy to Grace. "Your turn," she said.

Grace pressed Nutmeg close. She rubbed her cheek along Nutmeg's head. "Cheer up, little one," she said softly. "Everything will be all right." She gazed at the puppy. "Nutmeg is so pretty," she said. "Are all Cavalier King Charles spaniels this colour?"

Maya took on the role of a TV announcer, and

she pretended to hold a microphone up to Kat's mouth. "And now over to you, Einstein. Tell our audience, please, about the colours of King Charles spaniels."

Kat laughed. "Well, there are four colours of King Charles spaniels. Each has a different name." Kat put her finger on Nutmeg's little black nose. "You are a Blenheim King Charles spaniel. Chestnut and white," she told the puppy. "The black, chestnut-and-white spaniels are called tricolour King Charles. There are ruby King Charles, which are all chestnut, and there are the black-and-tan spaniels."

"And so that's it, folks!" Maya spoke into the microphone. "Yes, you heard it here live, on our popular show *Dog Breeds of the World,* with our very own Einstein."

As Kat and Grace laughed, Maya picked up a dog toy from the basket near the shelves. "Okay, time to show this puppy some fun!" she said.

"What do you say, Nutmeg? Do you want to play now?"

Maya shook the toy. "Look, Nutmeg! Look at this!" Maya threw the toy, which slid across the floor. "Want to get the toy, Nutmeg?"

Nutmeg lay in Grace's arms without moving. She wrinkled her nose and sighed.

"Oh, dear. There must be something wrong with her," Grace said.

"Let's not give up so soon," said Kat, taking the puppy from Grace's arms. "Listen, Nutmeg. You'll feel better if you play with us. Come on. Down you go."

She set the puppy on the floor, but Nutmeg just sat there. The puppy looked around the room, but she didn't move.

Maya picked up the dog toy that she had thrown across the room and she wiggled it on the floor, right in front of Nutmeg. "Oh, look, little puppy! Look at this! Get it, Nutmeg! Get the toy!"

The puppy's ears perked up. She pounced on the plush toy. She shook it back and forth in her mouth, making little growling noises.

Kat grinned. "That's more like it!"

Grace clapped her hands. "Bring it here, Nutmeg. Bring me the toy!" she called.

Nutmeg wagged her tail. Then she turned and ran toward the row of crates. She scooted behind a crate and stopped, peering back at the girls.

"Oh, here I come!" said Maya. "Like a big monster!" She bent low and slowly moved toward Nutmeg, swinging her arms.

Nutmeg's eyes opened wide. When Maya got close, Nutmeg scrambled out from her hiding place and raced away, still holding the toy in her mouth. Her eyes were sparkling.

Now Kat pretended to grab the toy. The tiny spaniel bounded away to the other side of the room. Then she set down the toy and barked excitedly.

The girls laughed. Kat was relieved that the puppy seemed all right.

For almost half an hour, the girls played with the puppy. They chased Nutmeg and she chased them. They rolled a ball back and forth between them, and Nutmeg raced after it. They set up two cardboard boxes end to end and put treats inside. They convinced Nutmeg to explore them. She even ate the treats.

Maya took some photos of Nutmeg playing. "You'll be in our Puppy Collection," she told the puppy. "We'll write about you, and we'll include these photos, too!"

But shortly after, Nutmeg stopped wagging her tail. The sparkle went out of her eyes. She didn't want to chase the ball anymore. She flopped down and put her head on her paws.

"Are you okay, Nutmeg?" Kat asked.

"She must be tired now after all this fun," said Grace.

Nutmeg napped for a while, but when she woke up, she still didn't want to play. The girls petted her while she lay quietly.

When it was time to leave, Kat gave the puppy a last kiss on the head. "Goodbye, Nutmeg," she told her, setting the little spaniel inside her crate. "Maybe you'll feel happier tomorrow."

"I'm sure she will," said Maya confidently.

But all that evening, long after she got home, Kat couldn't stop worrying.

CHAPTER FOUR

On Thursday the three girls hurried straight to Tails Up after school. Tony was at the front desk, chatting on the telephone. Marmalade was lying on the counter near him. Grace went over to say hello to the elderly cat.

There were three clients in the waiting room. A young man working on a laptop computer sat on one of the chairs. A woman sat on the couch with a white Great Pyrenees at her feet. He rested his huge head on the seat beside her, leaving no room for anyone else to sit on the couch.

"Look!" Maya said, nudging Kat. On another chair sat a man with sandy-brown hair in tight curls, a long nose and a pointed beard. At his feet sat an Airedale terrier. The dog had black-and-tan hair in tight curls. He had a long nose and a pointed beard.

"Another set of twins!" Kat giggled.

"Absolutely," agreed Maya.

Tony hung up the phone and waved Kat and Maya over.

"Hi, girls!" he said. "Jenn wonders if you can take Nutmeg to the park today."

"Sure," said Kat. "How's the puppy?"

Tony shook his head. "Not very lively. She's drinking water, but she hasn't touched her food today."

The smile faded from Kat's face. "Okay. Thanks, Tony," she said. Kat, Maya and Grace hurried to the doggy-daycare room. They saw the little King Charles spaniel puppy curled up in one of the four kennels along the wall.

"Hello, Nutmeg! Here we are!" cried Maya.

The puppy just lay there with her chin on her paws.

"Are you okay, puppy?" Kat asked, as she lifted Nutmeg out of the kennel. She held the tiny puppy against her chest. She could feel Nutmeg's heart beating against the palm of her hand. "Why won't you eat? What's wrong?"

Kat set Nutmeg down on some newspapers. When the puppy peed, Kat praised her and offered her a dog treat. Nutmeg sniffed at the treat, but she didn't take it.

Maya frowned. "That's not good," she said. "Puppies don't ever say no to treats!"

"Maybe she'll perk up at the park," said Grace. She pulled on one of her red braids. "Some fresh air and a good run might help."

As they walked to the park, Nutmeg seemed to cheer up. When they reached the park, the puppy lifted her head and sniffed the air. Along one side of the park were several rows of trees and bushes. There was a playground at one end of the park. At the other end was a hill with a grove of trees at the top. On one side of the hill was the town of Orchard Valley. On the other side was a small neighbourhood that opened out into fields.

"Okay, let's do some running," cried Grace. The girls raced across the wide open lawn toward the playground. Nutmeg trotted alongside. Her ears flew out behind her, and she held her tail high.

When they reached the playground, Nutmeg lay down, breathing hard. As the girls rested, they watched several boys throwing a football back and forth on the far side of the swings. Soon the puppy was back on her feet, looking around brightly.

"Ready to run again, Nutmeg?" suggested Maya. "Okay, let's go!"

Maya and Grace set off across the grass with the puppy, but Kat heard someone call her name. She turned. One of the boys was waving at her. It was Owen.

Kat gave a quick wave back. She was turning to catch up with Maya and Grace, but Owen kept waving. He jogged toward her.

"Hey," he said, when he got closer.

"Hi, Owen," said Kat quickly. "What's up?" Maya and Grace were getting farther and farther away. She thought about what Maya had said yesterday when she saw Kat chatting with Owen in the schoolyard: "I'm beginning to wonder if everyone's right, and you *do* like him." Now she was talking to Owen again!

"Nothing." Owen shrugged. His hat flaps dangled beside his ears. She and Maya had agreed that Owen looked like a basset hound in that hat. And he really did. Kat grinned thinking about it.

"I'm just here with Grace and Maya. We're helping my aunt look after a puppy." Kat pointed toward the girls. "So, I should . . ."

"We're just taking a break. From football,"

said Owen. "Me and Matt and Sunjit. That's the *we*."

"Right," said Kat. Again, she thought about what Maya said. But it seemed rude to just leave like this. Besides, she liked Owen. He was her friend.

"What kind of puppy is he? Or she?" asked Owen. He jammed his hands in his pockets.

"A Cavalier King Charles spaniel," Kat explained. "They're four different colours. They're . . ."

"Yeah, I know," Owen said.

"You do?" asked Kat, surprised. She thought back to the time their class had done research in the school library. She had gone straight to the animal section and looked at a book about dogs. Owen had come, too. But he had looked at a book about pigs and then one about birds. Not dogs.

Owen looked down at his feet. "Yeah. I've

been . . . doing some reading. About dogs. You know. Because I like . . ." Owen looked up at Kat. He looked back down at his feet again. ". . . dogs. Now. More now. More than before, I mean."

"Oh!" said Kat.

Owen was staring at her. "What's wrong?" he asked.

"Wrong?" she said.

"You look worried," Owen said.

"Oh, well . . ." Kat looked at Maya and Grace. They had stopped to wait for her. "I am a bit worried. About the puppy we're looking after — Nutmeg." Owen was listening closely. "She's not eating much. We're not sure why. We thought she'd feel better once she settled in. But now I'm not sure . . ."

Owen nodded. "Poor Nutmeg," he said.

"Yeah."

Kat waited for Owen to say she shouldn't worry and that the puppy would be all right. But he didn't. She sort of liked that.

"Anyway, I have to go," Kat said. "So, see you at school tomorrow, Owen." She gave him a wave. "Bye."

"Sorry," said Kat, when she caught up to Grace and Maya.

"That's okay," replied Grace cheerfully. "We were playing with Nutmeg while we waited."

Grace was holding one end of a stick. Nutmeg was tugging on the other end. The puppy had her tiny paws braced and her rear up in the air. She was growling as she pulled.

"Oh, Nutmeg, you're just too strong for me!" Grace said. She gently let go of the stick, and Nutmeg pranced away, the proud winner.

After the puppy finally dropped her prize,

Maya said, "Let's run with Nutmeg some more."

The girls raced along the field with Nutmeg several more times, letting her rest in between. Nutmeg even ate two of the nutritious dog treats they offered her. Next, they climbed to the top of the hill and let the puppy explore in the grove. Nutmeg barked at a squirrel and sniffed at some fallen logs. But then she seemed to lose interest.

They ran back down the hill to the field, but when they got to the bottom, Nutmeg stopped in her tracks and sat down. They waited, but she seemed too tired to go any farther.

"*Amigas*, I think we should head back to Tails Up with this little one," said Maya.

"Do you need to be carried, Nutmeg?" said Grace, scooping up the tiny spaniel. "I'll go first. We'll all take turns."

CHAPTER FIVE

The bell jingled as they entered the grooming salon through the front door. There weren't any dogs in the waiting room. Only one last client was there waiting for her dog.

Tony looked up from the computer and waved at the girls. "How's Nutmeg now?" he asked. "Did she cheer up at all?"

Marmalade lay on the counter near Tony. She was cleaning her paws, slowly and carefully.

"A little bit," said Kat, as she carried Nutmeg over.

"She liked running across the field," said Grace.

"And she ate some dog treats," added Maya.

"But you still look so sad, little one," said Tony, reaching out to pet the puppy.

As he did, Nutmeg began wiggling with excitement in Kat's arms. "Nutmeg seems really glad to see you, Tony!" Kat said, grinning.

"Nope, it's not me she's glad to see," said Tony. "Look! It's crabby old Marmalade."

Tony's right, Kat realized. Nutmeg was wagging her tail at Marmalade and struggling to get closer to her. Marmalade noticed, too. The tabby cat pulled her ears back. She glared at the spaniel and rose to her feet.

"Marmalade, you are so rude," Tony scolded. "You know what they say, girls. You can't teach an old cat new tricks!"

The girls laughed at Tony's joke.

Marmalade stepped away from the puppy, but then Nutmeg stopped wagging her tail. She whined softly.

Marmalade stopped. The cat's ears flicked forward and she looked steadily at the puppy. Nutmeg became very still. Again, she whined softly.

Suddenly, in one quick movement, Marmalade stretched her head forward — and gave the puppy a little kiss on the nose.

"Wow!" gasped Kat. Tony shook his head in amazement. Nutmeg gave a happy wag of her tail.

Then, satisfied, the elderly cat flicked her ears back and stalked away to the very end of the counter.

"Well, that's a first for Marmalade," said Tony. "This must be one special little puppy."

Tony gave Nutmeg a pat on the head, and then turned back to his work on the computer. Kat and the two girls took the puppy down the hallway to the doggy-daycare room.

"Nutmeg perked up there for a minute when Marmalade kissed her," said Kat. "But look at her now. She's sad again."

Nutmeg lay quietly in Kat's arms.

"Maybe she's just hungry," Grace said hopefully. "Her little tummy must be grumbling."

But when Kat tried setting the puppy down in front of her food bowl, she just looked up at Kat with her dark brown eyes. She didn't touch the food.

"Nutmeg," said Maya, worried. "You have to eat!" She crouched down beside the puppy and offered her another dog treat. Nutmeg sniffed it, but then she turned away.

It was difficult to leave her, but the girls knew they had to head home. Kat picked up Nutmeg and gave her one last cuddle. She kissed the top of the puppy's head and set her inside the kennel. "See you tomorrow, Nutmeg," she said. "Maybe you'll feel more at home here by then."

But deep down, Kat knew there was something else bothering Nutmeg. If she could just figure out what!

CHAPTER SIX

On Friday Kat and Maya had lunch at Kat's house.

"Not hungry?" Maya said, pointing to Kat's plate. Kat had hardly touched her sandwich. "You're as bad as Nutmeg!"

"Just worried about the puppy," said Kat.

"Why don't you call Tails Up and ask how she's doing?" suggested Maya.

"Good idea," said Kat. She headed for the

telephone and dialed the number.

Tony answered. "Nutmeg ate a little today — but not much," he told Kat. "But I had a little play with her this morning, and Jenn just took her out in the backyard on her lunch break. Oh, and she called Ms. Gulian, Nutmeg's owner," Tony added. "Jenn thinks Nutmeg might just be missing Ms. Gulian, but she wanted to ask her if she could think of anything else that might be upsetting the puppy. Aunt Jenn couldn't reach her, but she did leave a message."

"Thanks, Tony," said Kat. "Maya and Grace are busy after school today, but I'll be coming later to play with Nutmeg."

Soon Kat and Maya headed back to school. They met up with Grace in the schoolyard, and Maya told her what they had learned from Tony.

"Maybe Ms. Gulian will call back this afternoon," said Grace. "Maybe she'll know what's wrong."

"And today is Friday," said Maya. "So Nutmeg is only at Tails Up until Sunday. Two more days, then she'll be back in her own house again."

But nothing they said helped Kat to feel any better. All afternoon she worried about the spaniel puppy. When the final school bell rang, she was still worrying. She couldn't wait to get to Tails Up and spend some time with Nutmeg.

Kat knew that Maya had left school early for a dental appointment. Her mother was going to drop her off at Tails Up when she was done. Grace reminded Kat that she was off to visit her grandmother. "I'll see you and Maya tomorrow at Tails Up," Grace called, as she hurried down the hallway.

Kat zipped up her jacket and grabbed her backpack. *Nutmeg.*

"Are you okay, Kat?"

Kat looked up. Owen stood in front of her, looking concerned.

"Oh!" Kat shook her head. "I got distracted. No, I'm fine. I mean, yes. Yes, I'm okay."

Owen nodded slowly.

"I have to go. I'm going to Tails Up. There's a puppy there that . . ." Kat started moving toward the doors.

"Yes, you told me. At the park. Yesterday," Owen said. "It's Nutmeg, right? She's not very happy. She's not eating."

"That's right," Kat said quickly. "And I found out at lunch that she hasn't eaten today either." She swallowed hard. "And my aunt called the puppy's owner. She thought maybe she might know what's wrong. But Aunt Jenn couldn't reach her."

Owen nodded again. "I've been thinking . . ." He blushed. "Since yesterday. Since you told me about Nutmeg. I've been thinking about what you said."

Kat was surprised. She remembered what

Owen had said about liking dogs more now. It seemed he really did.

"Maybe Nutmeg is homesick," Owen went on.

"I thought of that," Kat interrupted. "But even if she were, what would we be able to do about it?"

"Well, did Nutmeg's owner leave anything at Tails Up to remind the puppy of home? A blanket? A favourite toy?"

"No," said Kat. "Nothing."

"I wonder if Nutmeg might cheer up if you just . . . took her to her house," said Owen. "I know you wouldn't be able to take her inside, but maybe she'd enjoy being in her own yard and smelling familiar smells. Do you think that might help?"

Kat smiled. "I don't know why I didn't think of that, Owen," she said. "It's a great idea. At least it's worth a try!"

Kat and Owen walked together out of the

school and across the yard. Owen pulled on his hat with the dangling ear flaps.

"Your Aunt Jenn will have Nutmeg's address, right?" asked Owen.

"For sure." Kat nodded. She gave him a quick hug. "Owen, you're the best. I'll see you later, okay?"

Owen didn't answer. When Kat glanced back, he was still standing there, but he was smiling.

Kat ran all the way to Tails Up. The bell on the door rang when she entered the waiting room.

A young woman sat on the couch working on a laptop. Two dogs lay side by side at her feet. One was a beautiful brown Labradoodle, a cross between a Labrador retriever and a poodle. The other was a black cockapoo, a cross between a cocker spaniel and a poodle. Both dogs had long, shaggy hair.

"You know your dogs can stay in our kennels until Jenn is ready for them," Tony said to the young woman. "That way, you wouldn't have to wait here."

"I suggested it, but I was out voted two to one," the young woman joked. "Besides, I brought some work to do."

Tony shook his head. "Dogs rule in Orchard Valley. No one in our whole town wants to kennel their dogs while they wait!" He winked at Kat.

Just then Maya hurried through the door. "No cavities," she said proudly, flashing a big smile, showing all her teeth.

Kat grinned and then quickly told Tony and Maya her plan to help Nutmeg cheer up. "Can you find Nutmeg's address for us?"

"Sure thing. Just give me a minute," said Tony.

"We'll go and get Nutmeg ready," Kat said cheerfully. She and Maya hurried into the doggy-daycare room.

"Nutmeg! Hello there!" Kat cooed.

"How are you, puppy?" said Maya.

The little King Charles spaniel puppy was curled up in a ball. She barely lifted her head when she heard the girls. "Nutmeg, you need to eat," Kat scolded, picking up the puppy. "Aren't you hungry today?"

She stroked the puppy's soft fur. She pulled gently on Nutmeg's silky ears. She breathed in her puppy smell.

"Well, maybe there's something Maya and I can do to get your appetite back," Kat said softly. "Come on. Let's go and find out!"

CHAPTER SEVEN

"We must be getting close to Nutmeg's house now," Maya said to Kat.

Tony had given the girls Nutmeg's address and drawn them a map. After they left Tails Up, they headed down the main street. Nutmeg trotted at the end of the leash. She sniffed at a fire hydrant. Her eyes went wide when a motorcycle roared past.

Soon after, the girls took her up a quieter

street, and a squirrel ran down a tree right in front of them. Nutmeg stopped and stared while the squirrel raced across a lawn and up another tree. As she watched, another squirrel raced after the first squirrel, and both squirrels disappeared into a leafy nest. Nutmeg raced over to sniff at the bottom of the tree. She barked three times.

"Oh, you're so brave now that the dangerous squirrels are gone," Maya teased the puppy. The girls were delighted to see Nutmeg so excited.

But after trotting along for another block, Nutmeg lay down. Kat and Maya waited patiently for her to jump back up again, but she didn't.

"Come on, Nutmeg," urged Kat. "Come on. Let's go. Come on, pup."

Nutmeg dropped her chin onto her paws and stared at the girls.

"Okey-dokey, then." Maya scooped up the puppy. "This afternoon, you get a free ride."

Kat looked down at the map. "We're getting close."

Soon, Kat looked up at the signpost at an intersection. "Here we are," she told the puppy. "Candlestick Lane."

The girls continued down the street, looking at the numbers on the houses. *123 Candlestick Lane . . . 125 Candlestick Lane . . . 127 . . . 129 . . .*

They stopped in front of 131 Candlestick Lane. It was a two-storey brick house with a wide front porch. The driveway was empty.

Kat set the puppy down. Nutmeg gave a big shake, beginning at her nose and working all the way to her tail.

"All set now, puppy?" Maya said, with a giggle.

Kat laughed, too. "Okay, now that you're

ready, Nutmeg, let's see if it cheers you up to be at your house!"

The girls walked the puppy up to the porch. She sniffed the bushes, and then pulled on her leash. She bounded up the steps.

Just then an elderly man with pure white hair came out the front door.

"Hello," he said to the girls, in a booming voice. "Hello, I'm Sam. Sam Mehta. How may I be of assistance?" Kat was just about to answer, but then Mr. Mehta noticed the puppy. "Oh, that's little Nutmeg, isn't it?" he went on. "Nice to see you, little one." He bent down and stroked the puppy's head. Again Kat was about to speak, but the man continued without taking a breath. "Tracy told me she was going out of town for several days, and she asked me to feed her cats. That's why I'm here now. I was doing just that."

Kat waited to see if the man had really finished. She tried not to catch Maya's eye

because she knew she might giggle.

After a moment, when she was certain Mr. Mehta was done speaking, she said, "I'm Kat, this is Maya, and you already know Nutmeg. Maya and I are helping my Aunt Jenn look after Nutmeg at Tails Up, where Nutmeg is boarding."

"I see," said Mr. Mehta, nodding. Then he frowned. "You know Tracy is away, of course.

So, why are you here with Nutmeg? Is everything okay? Is Nutmeg all right?"

"Well," said Kat, "Nutmeg isn't eating enough. She seems . . . well, she seems a bit sad. We think she might be homesick."

Just then, Nutmeg suddenly became alert. Her ears perked up. Her tail lifted. The spaniel puppy began pulling toward the front window. Kat saw the curtains moving.

A cat's face appeared in the window. Then the face of another cat appeared.

"Of course!" Kat said. "The two cats that live with Nutmeg!"

The puppy ran toward the window. She wagged her tail eagerly.

"Look how happy she is to see the cats!" Maya cried. Nutmeg gave a little bark. Kat picked up Nutmeg and held her close to the window. The spaniel pressed her little black nose to the glass. She wiggled with excitement.

"Maybe that's it," said Kat to Maya. "Nutmeg hasn't been homesick. She's been missing her cat friends!"

The two cats gazed back at the puppy. They blinked and twitched their whiskers. Then they turned and were gone. The curtains fell back into place.

Immediately Nutmeg's tail drooped. She waited, staring at the window, but the cats didn't return.

"That's it for sure," agreed Maya. "Nutmeg misses her cats."

"Well then, I have the perfect solution," said Mr. Mehta. "I have an appointment right now, but tomorrow . . . Why don't you ask your parents if you they can bring you and Nutmeg by tomorrow at about this same time? I'll let you all in and Nutmeg can have a visit with her cats. I know Tracy wouldn't mind. In fact, I'm sure she'd be grateful to you."

Kat and Maya grinned at each other [...] at Mr. Mehta. "That would be wonderi[...] Kat.

"Just *purrr*fect," said Maya, with a spa[...] her eyes.

CHAPTER EIGHT

By the time Kat and Maya got back to Tails Up, the waiting room was empty. Kat heard Aunt Jenn's voice coming from the grooming studio. She knocked and poked her head around the door.

"Kitty-Kat!" said Aunt Jenn. "Come in!" She was sweeping the room and chatting with Tony. Tony held Marmalade in his arms. He was gently stroking his big tabby cat, and as usual,

Marmalade was pretending not to enjoy the attention.

"Kat, Tony tells me you went to Nutmeg's house," said Aunt Jenn.

"I wondered if Nutmeg might be homesick. I hoped she might cheer up if she could visit her house and maybe play in her yard," Kat began.

"It was a clever idea," said Aunt Jenn.

Kat wanted to explain that it wasn't her idea, that it was Owen's idea. But suddenly the thought of saying his name aloud made her feel awkward.

Aunt Jenn started laughing. "Look at you, Nutmeg! Why are you suddenly so excited?" Nutmeg was squirming in Kat's arms. She wagged her tail and her ears perked up.

"Nutmeg likes cats!" Maya said. "She acted like this yesterday when she saw Marmalade."

As Kat brought Nutmeg closer to Marmalade, the puppy continued to wag her tail.

"And believe it or not," Tony said to Aunt Jenn, "this grumpy old thing seems to have a soft spot for Nutmeg." He moved toward Kat and Nutmeg. This time Marmalade didn't put her ears back. She didn't glare at the puppy.

Aunt Jenn stopped sweeping to see what would happen.

The cat cautiously stretched out her foreleg and gave Nutmeg a gentle little swat on the ear. Nutmeg wiggled happily at the cat's affectionate tap.

"Well, isn't that something!" said Aunt Jenn, surprised. Then she thought for a moment. "Maybe Marmalade could help cheer up Nutmeg! Could she spend some time with the puppy tomorrow, Tony?"

Tony shook his head. "I don't think it would work," he said regretfully. "Just look."

Looking pleased with herself, Marmalade settled back into Tony's arms. She resumed

ignoring the four humans and arched her back, signalling to Tony that he could return to stroking her.

"Marmalade seems to want to console Nutmeg," Tony continued, "but it looks like one little cat pat or kiss is all this old gal can manage at a time!"

"I guess you're right," said Aunt Jenn, with a sigh.

"But it might be okay," said Kat quickly. "Just now, when we were at Nutmeg's house, she got really excited when she saw Tracy's two cats through the window. *Really* excited! We think she misses the cats!"

"And we met Tracy's neighbour, Mr. Mehta, the one who is feeding Tracy's cats," said Maya. "He invited us to bring Nutmeg back tomorrow so she can play with her cats!"

"That sounds like it might be very helpful," said Aunt Jenn. Kat saw the worry in her aunt's eyes as she looked at the puppy. "I hope that will cheer up our sweet little Nutmeg. Ms. Gulian isn't coming back until Sunday morning, and we might not hear from her before then. That's a long time for a little Cavalier King Charles puppy to be so sad. It's a long time for her to go without eating very much."

Kat's eyes filled with tears. She bent her head over the puppy.

"Don't worry. Everything will be okay," she whispered. But really, she wasn't certain at all.

CHAPTER NINE

Kat had just finished dinner with her family. Grinning from ear to ear, she phoned Maya and Grace to explain the plan for tomorrow. She arranged to meet the girls at Tails Up in the morning to play with Nutmeg.

"We'll walk over to Candlestick Lane in the afternoon, just like Mr. Mehta suggested. Dad will meet us there," she explained. "I hope Nutmeg will cheer up when she sees her cat buddies!"

Kat also invited the girls to her house afterwards for dinner and to work on the Puppy Collection. Maya and Grace were each very excited to accept Kat's invitation.

Kat, Grace and Maya arrived at Tails Up on Saturday morning and hurried directly into the doggy-daycare room. Nutmeg lay in her kennel under the window.

"Nutmeg, guess who you're going to see this afternoon?" called Maya.

The puppy looked up and gave a few wags of her tail. Then she put her head down again.

With a grin, Kat lifted the puppy out of the kennel. She held Nutmeg close. Her fur was so soft. Her puppy smell was so sweet! "Oh, Nutmeg," Kat said. "I know you'll cheer up when you see your cat pals. But for now, let's have some fun in the backyard."

The yard behind Tails Up was enclosed by a

chain-link fence. There were trees along one side and a garden down the other side.

The day was cool, but the sun was bright. All morning long, the girls encouraged Nutmeg to play. They threw toys for the puppy but ended up fetching most of the toys themselves. They ran around the yard but ended up chasing each other more than the puppy chased them.

At noon, the girls took Nutmeg back inside. They ate the lunches they had brought. As they finished up, Maya looked at the puppy's food bowl. "Nutmeg hasn't touched her breakfast," Maya said, frowning.

"You're right," said Grace. Then she smiled. "I know! Let's take some of Nutmeg's food with us to her house. We can try to feed her there. Maybe she'll get her appetite back when she's with the cats."

Maya put some puppy food into her backpack while Kat put the dog toys away. Grace clipped Nutmeg's leash to her collar.

The girls waved goodbye to Tony as they left the grooming salon. As they headed down the main street of Orchard Valley, Nutmeg trotted along beside them. Many passersby stopped and asked to pet the beautiful puppy.

"Oh, what a beautiful Cavalier King Charles spaniel," said one man. "I once had one named Dolly. A Blenheim too, like yours. Have you considered showing this little gal when she's a bit older? Although," the man paused, "she might not be well-suited for the ring." He bent down and stroked Nutmeg. "Your puppy doesn't seem to have quite enough of a spark, if you'll pardon me for saying so. She's lovely, but she seems a bit . . . subdued."

"Subdued," repeated Grace, as they walked on. "I don't know that word. What does *subdued* mean?"

Maya shrugged. "Don't know," she said. She took an explorer's pose, peering ahead into the distance, with her hand shading her eyes. "Our destination lies this-a-way," she said, in a gruff voice. "Onward go the three *amigas*!"

"Subdued?" Kat grinned at Grace. "Picture Maya . . ."

"Maya is subdued?" asked Grace.

"Nope," continued Kat. "Picture Maya — and then picture someone the exact *opposite* of Maya. That is subdued! Subdued means low-key. Like when you turn down the volume on music."

Grace giggled. "And Maya is like when you turn up the volume!"

"Exactly," said Kat. She scooped up Nutmeg. "You're subdued now, little Nutmeg, but what will you be like when we get you home again?"

About fifteen minutes later, Kat called out, "There it is. 131 Candlestick Lane. That's Nutmeg's house." She pointed. "Mr. Mehta lives on that side." Then Kat waved. "And there's my dad. On time, as usual!"

Kat's dad waved back. At the same time, Mr. Mehta came out of his house.

"Hello! Hello!" he called to Kat and Maya. "I'm Sam Mehta," he told Kat's father and Grace as he came down his front walkway, "and I'm so glad you have brought little Nutmeg by."

"This is my friend Grace and my father, Robert Reynolds," said Kat.

Everyone said hello and then headed down the walkway to 131 Candlestick Lane. "I've been coming over twice a day while Tracy is away," Mr. Mehta explained. "I feed the cats in the morning. I also come by in the afternoon to say hello to them."

As they approached the house, Kat saw the curtains in the front window move. She saw the flicker of a black tail. Kat whispered to Nutmeg, "Your buddies are waiting!"

"Some of Nutmeg's toys are in the kitchen," Mr. Mehta said, as he unlocked the door. "Her water bowl is there, too." The girls and Mr. Reynolds followed him inside.

"Oh, look!" said Maya. "There are the cats!"

Two cats stood on the back of the couch, which was up against the front window. One cat was black and white with a white-tipped tail. The other cat was grey and white. They looked with interest at their guests.

"The black cat is Oliver. The grey cat is Buddy," explained Mr. Mehta. "They are young cats and lots of fun. I'll come back in an hour and a half to lock up. Does that give you enough time here?"

"That will be great. Thanks," said Kat.

With a wave, Mr. Mehta was gone.

CHAPTER TEN

"This little puppy doesn't seem to be sad in the slightest!" remarked Kat's father, with a grin.

"I've never seen Nutmeg so excited!" Grace cried.

The puppy was squirming in Kat's arms, struggling to get down. Kat unclipped the leash and set Nutmeg on the floor. She was off in a flash, running across the living room toward the cats.

The puppy reached the couch and tried to jump up, but she was too small. She yipped excitedly, wagging her tail.

Oliver and Buddy jumped down onto the seat of the couch. Buddy made a sound between a meow and a purr. The grey cat lowered his paw and playfully batted at the puppy's nose.

Nutmeg wagged her tail even harder. She stood with her front paws up on the side of the couch and gave Buddy's paw a gentle nip.

"This is amazing," cried Maya.

The black cat jumped from the couch to the floor. Tail in the air, Oliver studied the puppy as she bounced toward him. He waited until Nutmeg was almost upon him. Then he sprang into the dining room. The spaniel puppy flew after the cat, her ears flying.

Kat giggled. "Oliver is almost twice as big as Nutmeg!"

The girls watched as the cat led the puppy

around and around the legs of the dining-room table and its six chairs. Kat and Grace each perched on a living-room chair, watching the game. Maya snapped photos with her camera. Kat's father watched for a while, and then he settled into reading the weekend newspaper.

"Nutmeg is going to be exhausted by all the fun!" Kat exclaimed.

Just then, Oliver darted across the living room with Nutmeg tearing after him. The cat leaped back up onto the back of the couch and casually lay down. Nutmeg sat at the foot of the couch, her tongue hanging out, panting happily.

The puppy had only rested for a few minutes when Buddy jumped down from the couch. Looking right at Nutmeg, the grey cat lay down and then rolled over onto his back. The puppy scrambled to her feet and approached the cat. Wagging her tail, Nutmeg sniffed at Buddy's belly. The cat waved his legs in the air and pretended to box at the puppy's nose. Nutmeg sat down and cheerfully poked at Buddy with her nose. Buddy batted at Nutmeg again.

Suddenly Buddy jumped up and darted behind the couch. Nutmeg tore after him. The girls laughed as the cat bounded out from the other side of the couch and ran under Kat's chair.

"Wow!" giggled Kat, raising her feet out of Nutmeg's way as the puppy bounded after the cat.

Buddy did a few more laps of the room with Nutmeg in close pursuit.

The grey cat came to a halt in the middle of the living-room floor and flopped down onto his side. The puppy collapsed in a heap right beside him. Nutmeg poked at Buddy with her nose a few times, and he batted his paw back at her. Then the puppy and the cat both fell asleep.

The three girls smiled at one another. "Nutmeg is having the best time," said Maya.

"Let's put out some of her food now," said Grace.

"Okay," agreed Kat. "It would be great if we could get her to eat something while she's here."

The girls went into the kitchen. Maya took the dog food and Nutmeg's bowl from her backpack. She and Grace put some food in the bowl, and Kat filled another bowl with water for the puppy.

Kat spotted a dog bed by the kitchen window. "This must be Nutmeg's," said Kat. "Here are some dog toys, too." She squeezed one of the toys, and it made a squeaky noise. Nutmeg raced into the kitchen, her eyes sparkling.

Kat squeezed the toy again, and Nutmeg looked up at it, wagging her tail. Kat threw the toy across the kitchen floor and Nutmeg raced after it. The puppy picked up the toy and ran back into the living room with it.

The girls laughed and followed her. Nutmeg dropped the toy beside Buddy, who batted at it with one paw. Oliver leaped down from the couch and pounced on the toy. Nutmeg put her head down and her rear end in the air. Pretending to be fierce, she made a little growl. Then she grabbed at the toy. She ran off with it, the cats chasing her.

The puppy and the two cats continued to play until Nutmeg was tired. Once more she fell asleep, this time cuddling with Oliver.

When the puppy woke up from her short nap, Grace carried her into the kitchen and set her down in front of the bowls. Nutmeg drank thirstily. Then she looked at her food.

Kat held her breath.

Nutmeg began to eat. Maya, Grace and Kat exchanged looks. None of them dared to speak. They didn't want to risk distracting the puppy.

Nutmeg ate and ate and ate. She ate until the bowl was empty. She had another small drink of water. Then she went to her dog bed, curled up in it and dropped back to sleep.

"Thank goodness!" said Grace.

"This is the first time Nutmeg has had a full tummy in days," said Maya.

Kat sighed with relief.

When Nutmeg woke up, she had more fun with the cats. The puppy and the cats wrestled and ran. They chased one another. They played hide-and-seek.

When Mr. Mehta returned, the girls couldn't believe it was already time to head home. Kat's father folded up the newspaper, and Grace clipped the leash onto Nutmeg's collar.

The girls said goodbye to Mr. Mehta, and Kat gave her father a big thank-you hug. Then Kat and her friends walked back to Tails Up with Nutmeg. When they were in the doggy-daycare room, Grace rubbed the puppy's silky ears for the last time. "Goodbye, little Nutmeg," she said.

"I'll miss you," Maya told the puppy.

"So will I," Kat said. She gave the puppy a kiss on her head, and Grace set her into the kennel.

Kat's heart was heavy, but she reminded herself that Nutmeg wasn't sick and she wasn't refusing to eat anymore. Kat smiled as she thought about how much happier Nutmeg would be in her own home with her cat friends.

CHAPTER ELEVEN

"How's this?" said Maya. She, Grace and Kat were sitting on the floor in Kat's bedroom.

Kat was drawing pictures of Nutmeg to put in the Puppy Collection scrapbook. Grace was sorting through photos of the puppy.

Maya read aloud: *"Nutmeg is ten weeks old. She is a Cavalier King Charles spaniel puppy. Her colour is Blenheim, which is chestnut and white. She is very sweet, and she loves her cat friends. When she is on her own, she is subdued. When she is with her cat friends, she is dramatic, energetic and outgoing!"*

"Perfect," said Grace.

"Nice one." Kat grinned and gave Maya a thumbs-up.

"It was so much fun seeing how happy Nutmeg was with her cat friends," said Grace. "I'm so glad you thought of taking the puppy to visit them, Kat."

Kat bent over her drawing. "It wasn't my idea," she mumbled.

"Pardon?" asked Grace.

"It wasn't my idea," said Kat, speaking more clearly.

Maya looked up from her notepad. "No? Whose idea was it?" she asked.

Kat blushed.

"Kat-nip?" asked Maya. She set down her pencil. Grace put down the photos.

"It was Owen's idea," Kat said. "I ran into him after school yesterday. I was worried about Nutmeg, and it all sort of spilled out. He is my friend, after all. There's no reason I shouldn't talk to him about Nutmeg. He actually really likes dogs."

Maya and Grace didn't say anything. They just smiled at each other.

"What?" Kat said. She put her hands on her hips. She frowned. "What's so funny?"

"Nothing," said Grace, with an innocent look on her face.

"Nothing," said Maya, with an equally innocent look on her face.

"I don't *like* him," protested Kat. She wasn't sure why, but her face was red. "He's not my boyfriend. And he doesn't have lovey-dovey eyes."

"Okay," said Maya.

"Okay," said Grace.

"Although he did have a good idea about how to help Nutmeg," said Maya. She picked up her pencil and began writing.

Grace began sorting through the photos again. "So if you did like him, it wouldn't be a big deal."

"Okay," said Kat. She felt herself calm down. She felt her face returning to normal.

As she continued her sketch of Nutmeg, she thought about the sweet puppy. Nutmeg had been so lonely without Oliver and Buddy. Her two cat friends were so important to the little spaniel.

Kat looked over at Maya and Grace. She felt the same way about her two friends.

I'm so lucky! she thought. *I can help look after puppies like Nutmeg at Tails Up. Plus, I have the two best friends in the whole wide world!*